LAURA CECIL

NOAH
and the
SPACE
ARK

Illustrated by

EMMA CHICHESTER CLARK

PUFFIN BOOKS

Many many years from now Earth was very crowded. It was crammed with people, buildings, machines and space ships. There were no forests or big animals left: no elephants, no rhinos, giraffes or tigers.

There was only room for small animals.
They all lived in a park where the last
trees and flowers grew.

The park was looked after by Noah and
Mrs Noah with their three sons, Ham,
Shem and Japhet and their families.

Every day Noah cared for the plants and trees.
All the animals looked forward to his visits.

WHERE ARE THEY NOW ?

EXTINCT

If they were ill he
looked after them. His
grandchildren Hannah
and Sam helped him.

Then one year there was no rain. The sky was dark and smoky. The trees and plants drooped and would not grow and the animals could not find enough to eat.

The next year there was still no rain. It grew stiflingly hot. One morning Noah found a little bird gasping for breath.

The next day he found more sick animals.

Noah called the family together. "This is a warning,"
he said. "We cannot stay on Earth.
We must build a space ship and find a new planet to live on."
"We must take the animals!" cried Sam and Hannah.
"Of course," said Mrs Noah, "and we'll take plants and seeds too."

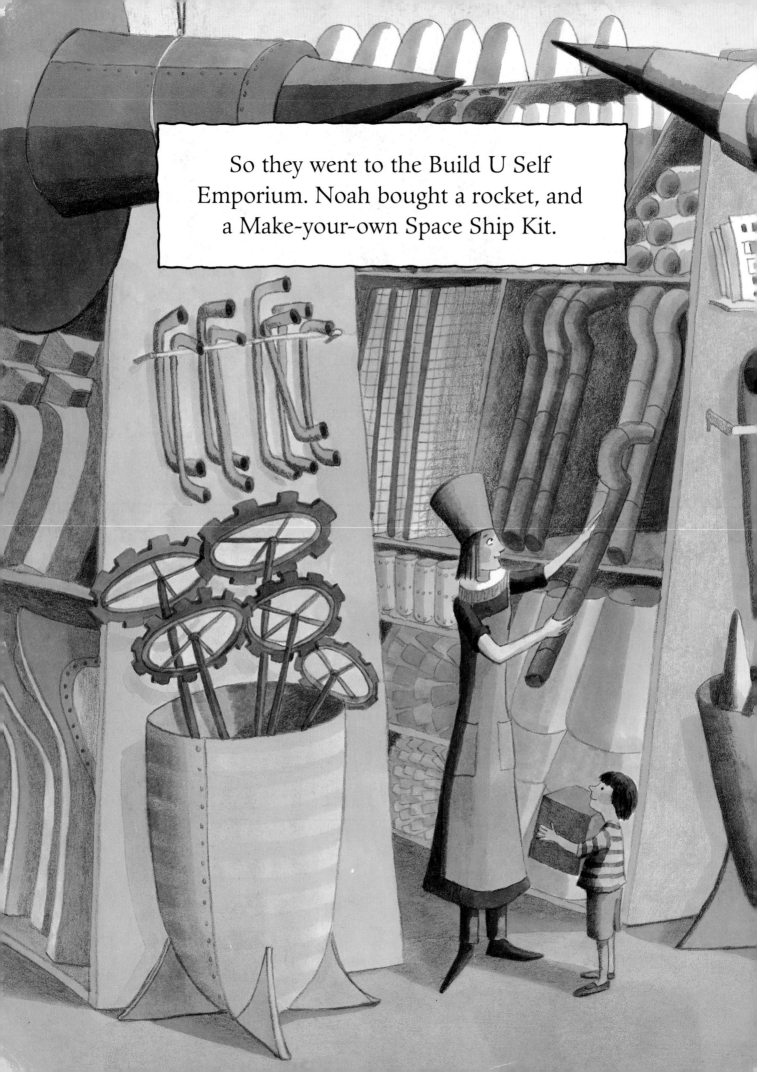

So they went to the Build U Self
Emporium. Noah bought a rocket, and
a Make-your-own Space Ship Kit.

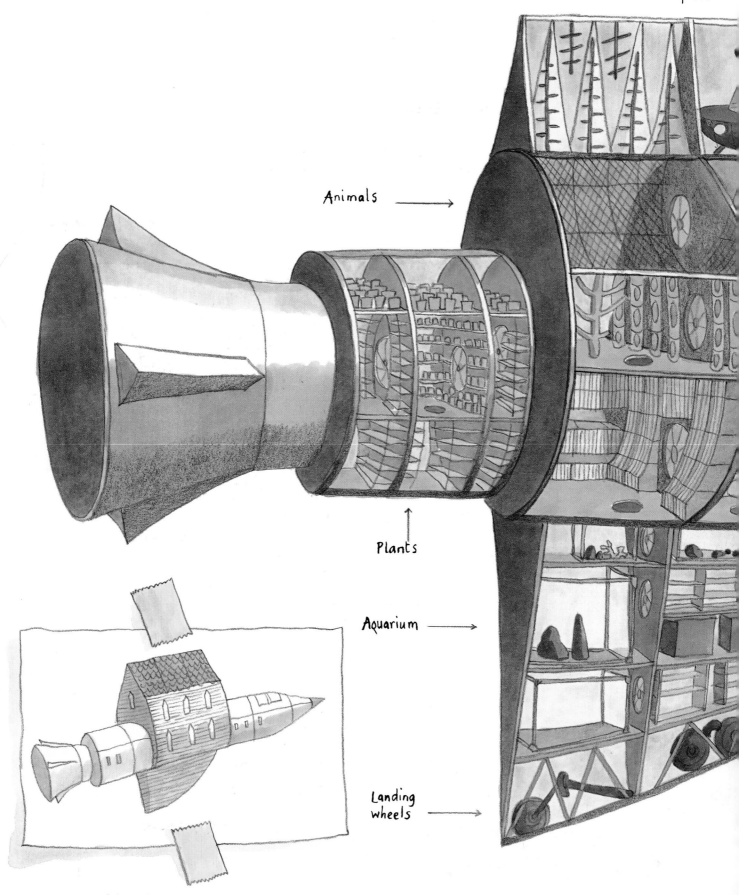

Space
probe

Animals →

↑
Plants

Aquarium →

Landing
wheels →

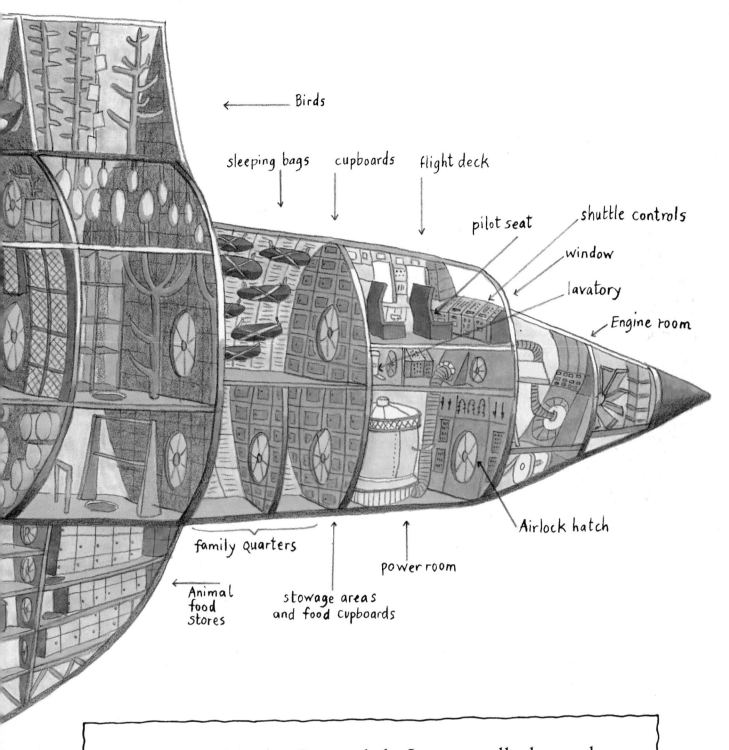

Birds

sleeping bags   cupboards   flight deck

pilot seat   shuttle controls

window

lavatory

Engine room

family quarters

power room

Airlock hatch

Animal
food
stores

stowage areas
and food cupboards

He called it the Space Ark. It was well planned.
The smaller section at the front was for Noah's
family. The middle section was for the animals,
and the plants were stored at the back.

Mrs Noah prepared the plants
and trees for the journey.

When people heard about the Space Ark
they crowded round to have a look.

Noah was interviewed on television. Everyone laughed when he told them why he was building the Space Ark.

But day after day it grew warmer and warmer and the air grew thicker and smokier.

By the time the Space Ark was ready, it was unbearably hot and they could hardly breathe. "We must leave now!" cried Noah. "Go and find all the animals and get them on board quickly!"

Some of the animals came at once,

but some were asleep.

Others hid in unexpected places.

At last they all climbed aboard two by two.

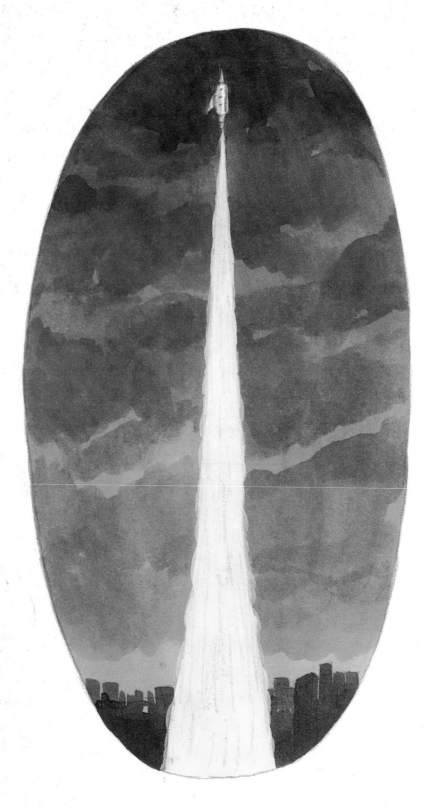

Noah counted: "Ten, nine, eight, seven,
six, five, four, three, two, one, LIFT OFF!"

There was a roar as the rocket engines fired up.
Then the Space Ark vanished into the sky.

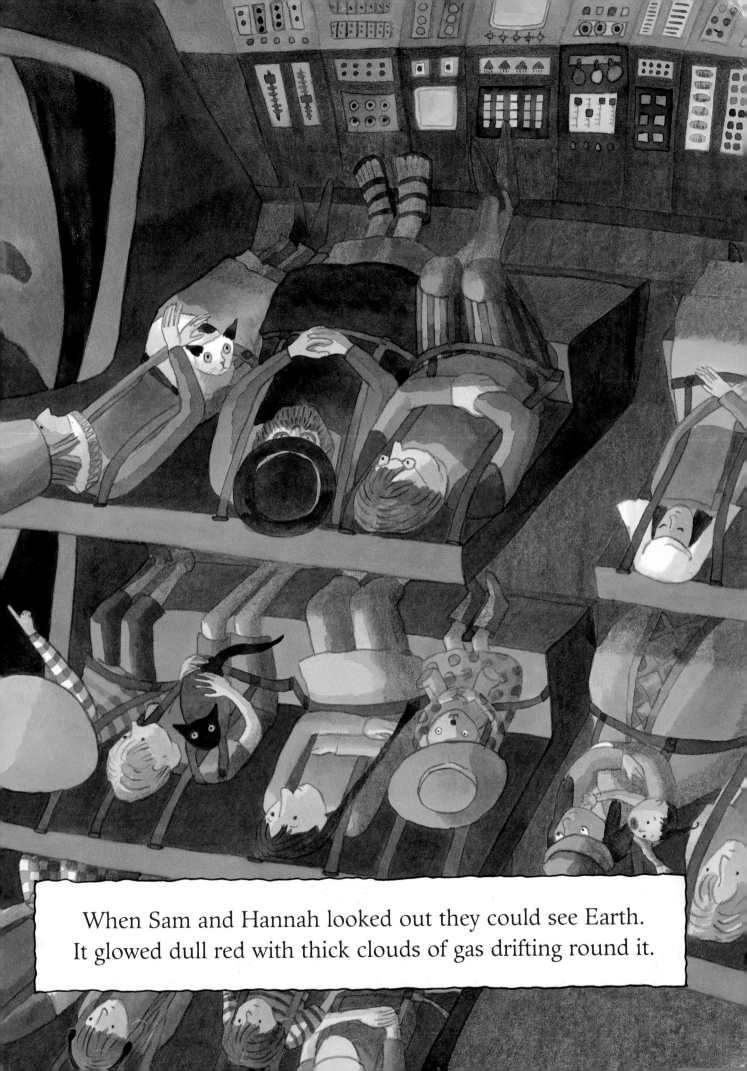

When Sam and Hannah looked out they could see Earth.
It glowed dull red with thick clouds of gas drifting round it.

Now they were up in space,
everything became weightless.
There was no up or down.

Everyone had to get used to floating.

Some of the animals didn't enjoy this.

Neither did Mrs. Noah.

For forty days and forty nights the Ark travelled through space looking for a new planet. Then they saw a beautiful blue and green world shining in front of them. "We'll try there," said Noah.

Ham and Mrs. Noah went ahead in a space probe.

They needed to test the air on the planet to see if it was safe to breathe.

Seven days passed. Everyone waited anxiously
for their return. Then Ham and Mrs Noah were
back, full of excitement. It was safe to land!

Noah put the Space Ark into a steep dive.

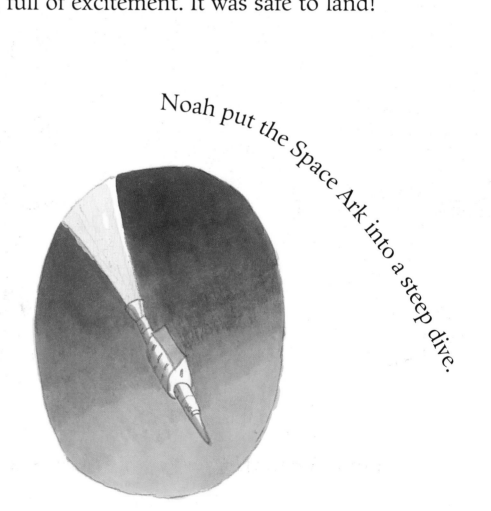

They landed on the planet with a judder and
a bump. When they looked out they were amazed.

There were animals and trees everywhere
and a huge rainbow shone across the sky.
Hannah took a deep breath of fresh air. "It looks
like a picture in one of your old history books,
Grandfather," she said.
"We have found our new home," said Noah.

For Caspar and Cosima - L.C.
For Josie - E.C.C.

HAMISH HAMILTON/PUFFIN

Published by the Penguin Group
Penguin Books Ltd, 27 Wrights Lane, London W8 5TZ, England
Penguin Putnam Inc., 375 Hudson Street, New York, New York 10014, USA
Penguin Books Australia Ltd, Ringwood, Victoria, Australia
Penguin Books Canada Ltd, 10 Alcorn Avenue, Toronto, Ontario, Canada M4V 3B2
Penguin Books (NZ) Ltd, Private Bag 102902, NSMC, Auckland, New Zealand

Penguin Books Ltd, Registered Offices: Harmondsworth, Middlesex, England

First published by Hamish Hamilton Ltd 1997
1 3 5 7 9 10 8 6 4 2

Published in Picture Puffins 1998
3 5 7 9 10 8 6 4

Text copyright © Laura Cecil, 1997
Illustrations copyright © Emma Chichester Clark, 1997

The moral right of the author and illustrator has been asserted

Made and printed in Italy by Printer Trento Srl

British Library Cataloguing in Publication Data
A CIP catalogue record for this book is available from the British Library

ISBN 0–241–13680–6 Hardback
ISBN 0–140–55912–4 Paperback